A Note to Parents

Reading books aloud and playing word games are two valuable ways parents can help their children learn to read. The easy-to-read stories in the **My First Hello Reader! With Flash Cards** series are designed to be enjoyed together. Six activity pages and 16 flash cards in each book help reinforce phonics, sight vocabulary, reading comprehension, and facility with language. Here are some ideas to develop your youngster's reading skills:

Reading With Your Child

- Read the story aloud to your child and look at the colorful illustrations together. Talk about the characters, setting, action, and descriptions. Help your child link the story to events in his or her own life.
- Read parts of the story and invite your child to fill in the missing parts. At first, pause to let your child "read" important last words in a line. Gradually, let your child supply more and more words or phrases. Then take turns reading every other line until your child can read the book independently.

Enjoying the Activity Pages

- Treat each activity as a game to be played for fun. Allow plenty of time to play.
- Read the introductory information aloud and make sure your child understands the directions.

Using the Flash Cards

- Read the words aloud with your child. Talk about the letters and sounds and meanings.
- Match the words on the flash cards with the words in the story.
- Help your child find words that begin with the same letter and sound, words that rhyme, and words with the same ending sound.
- Challenge your child to put flash cards together to make sentences from the story and create new sentences.

Above all else, make reading time together a fun time. Show your child that reading is a pleasant and meaningful activity. Be generous with your praise and know that, as your child's first and most important teacher, you are contributing immensely to his or her command of the printed word.

—Tina Thoburn, Ed.D.
Consultant

D1124679

Library of Congress Cataloging-in-Publication Data

Christensen, Nancy.
 Who am I? / by Nancy Christensen ; illustrated by Rowan Barnes-Murphy.
    p.   cm.
 Summary: Rhyming text provides clues about the nature of the animal who is speaking.
 ISBN 0-590-46192-3
 [1. Animals—Fiction.   2. Literary recreations.   3. Stories in rhyme.]   I. Barnes-Murphy, Rowan, ill.   II. Title.
 PZ8.3.C4565Wh   1993
 [E]—dc20   92-36006
                                                                         CIP
                                                                         AC

12   11   10   9   8   4   5   6   7   8/9

Printed in the U.S.A.   24

First Scholastic printing, September 1993

WHO AM I?

by Nancy Christensen
Illustrated by Rowan Barnes-Murphy

My First Hello Reader!
With Flash Cards

SCHOLASTIC INC. Cartwheel ·B·O·O·K·S· TM

New York   Toronto   London   Auckland   Sydney

I am not tall.

I am not small.

I have not any spots at all.

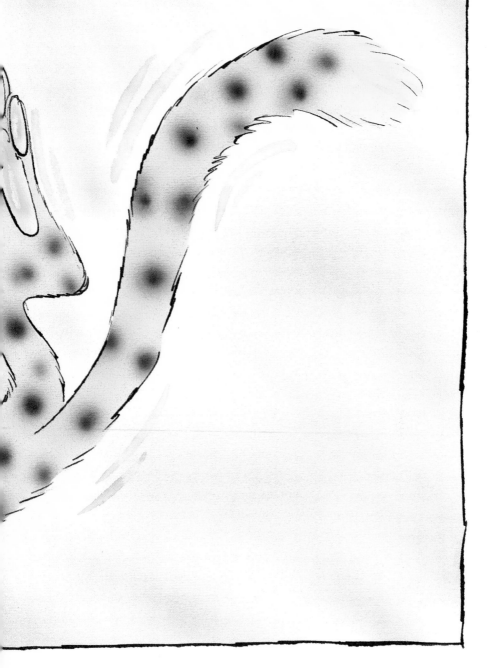

I have no hat.

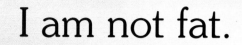

I am not fat.

I do not have
a baseball bat.

I	am
not	tall
no	hat
swim	fat

any	have
spots	small
at	all
I	do

way	up
but	fly
you	can
find	me

cannot	bat
who	high
not	meow
a	baseball

I cannot swim.

I cannot fly.

But you can find me
way up high.

I am not small.
I am not tall.

I am not fat.
I have no hat.

Who am I?

Meow.

Rhyming Words

Some of the words in this story rhyme.

small, tall, all
hat, fat, bat
fly, high, I

Look at the words and pictures in each row. Point to the picture that rhymes with each word.

small

hat

fly

tall

fat

high

Who Says?

Point to the picture of the animal that said *meow* in this story.

What if, instead of *meow*, the last word in the story was *woof*? Which animal says *woof*?

Match these sounds to the animals that make these noises:

oink

roar

tweet

moo

neigh

Can You Guess Who I Am?

Read the sentences below. Who am I?

My shirt is not red.
I am not wearing a tie.
My buttons are not red.
I am not wearing stripes.

Point to me.

Big or Small?

Is the animal in this picture big or small?

Fancy or plain?

What are some words that describe what she *is*?

What are some words that describe what she *is not*?

The Opposite

Opposites are words that mean something completely different. *Small* and *tall* are opposites. *Fat* and *thin* are, too.

Look at the pictures below. Can you point to the picture in each row that is the opposite of the first picture?

cold / hot

open / closed

many / few

old / young

fast / slow

noisy / quiet

The Same

Sometimes words mean the same thing as other words. You can use the word *small* and the word *little* to mean the same thing. *Fat* and *heavy* can mean the same thing, too.

Look at the words below. Can you pick out which word in each row means the same thing as the first word?

cold   chilly, big, open

closed   open, shut, small

many   lots, loud, little

old   young, fast, aged

fast   tall, first, quick

noisy   secret, loud, old

Answers

(Rhyming Words)

small   **hat**   **fly**

tall   **fat**   **high**

(Who Says?)

oink **roar** **tweet** **moo** **neigh**

(Can You Guess Who I Am?)

(Big or Small?)

big **fancy**

Answers will vary.

(The Opposite)

hot   **few**   **slow**

closed   **young**   **quiet**

(The Same)

chilly, shut, lots, aged, quick, loud